Beading Techniques

Reader's Digest

The Reader's Digest Association, Inc.
Pleasantville, New York/Monteal/Sydney/Hong Kong

Contents

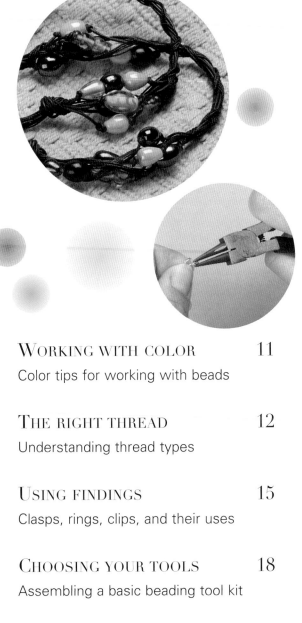

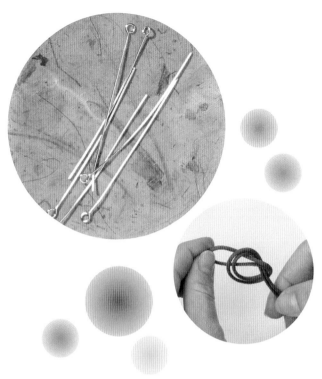

Introduction

For thousands of years, beads have been used across most continents for adornment, in prayer, and even for barter. Current fashion trends mean beading crafts have enjoyed a surge in popularity, and an almost bewildering variety of affordable and attractive beads are now widely available.

Across Africa, India, North America, the Middle East, and much of Europe, beads have been strung, woven, and even occasionally used as currency. From ancient Mesopotamia to the modern shopping mall, they have added their sparkle to otherwise ordinary items.

Beads are normally inexpensive to buy and require little in the way of storage or work space. As this book demonstrates, to produce attractive beadwork, you don't need any expensive, specialized equipment or a lot of time or effort.

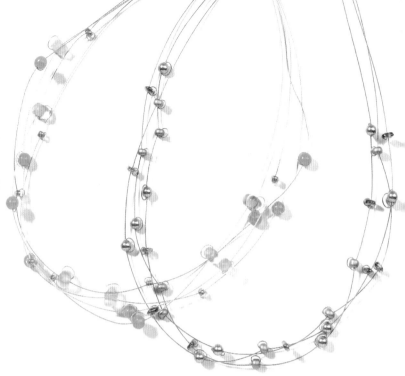

Collecting beads, finding them in unexpected places, and making them from found objects or household items can be a rewarding hobby in itself. For some suggestions for beads you might like to collect or make, see page 38.

One of the beauties of beading is that the items you make are almost indefinitely reusable. When a pattern palls or becomes outdated, you can simply undo the beadwork and use the beads in a different way.

In this book and the accompanying book, *Beading Projects*, you will find simple, easy-to-use instructions that will enable you to create beautiful and useful items that will be a pleasure to own and use for years to come.

We haven't attempted to cover every aspect of this fascinating craft and have chosen to describe the simplest method of achieving our objective wherever possible. In no time at all, you will be able to design and create your own unique projects.

What's in your kit

The materials in your kit will enable you to experiment with the techniques described in this book and to complete several projects. As you gain experience, you will find your preferred methods and assemble your own unique collection of materials and tools.

In the kit you will find everything you need to start beading—sufficient beads, threads, and findings to complete your first projects and allow you to try out a few of your own ideas.

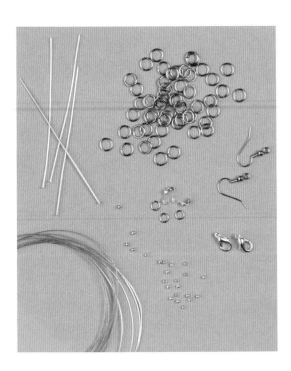

Your complete kit contains:

1. 2 x 5-mm silver carab clasps, which are an attractive way to fasten jewelry.

2. 3 x 5-mm silver jump rings for attaching findings (see page 16).

3. 2 small calottes to hide unsightly crimp beads and knots, and allow you to add fastenings to your jewelry.

4. 50 split rings to hold findings and beads, for the charm bracelet. See the *Beading Projects* book, on pages 6–9.

5. 2 shepherd's hook earring wires, which are used to make the earrings described in the *Beading Projects* book, on pages 42–45.

6. 4 headpins, also used for the earrings in the *Beading Projects* book, on pages 42–45.

7. 20 crimp beads, which you will use in most projects, to hold beads and findings in place on the thread.

8. 5 ft. (1.5 m) of tigertail—a nylon-covered wire used for the floating necklace in your *Beading Projects* book, on pages 18–21.

9. 3 ft. (90 cm) of medium-weight wire, for fixing beads to your charm bracelet and for use in many other jewelry projects.

10. For the earrings on pages 39–45 in the *Beading Projects* book, the kit includes 2 long and 6 short bugle beads, 2 larger faceted beads, and 6 small faceted beads.

11. For the charm bracelet, the kit includes 6 specialty beads and over 15 small beads.

12. For the floating necklace, the kit includes 21 square beads.

13. A packet of seed beads, which are used for various projects.

14. The plastic tray containing the various elements of kit is a useful bead board, with wells to hold beads while you are working and channels for planning necklace sequences.

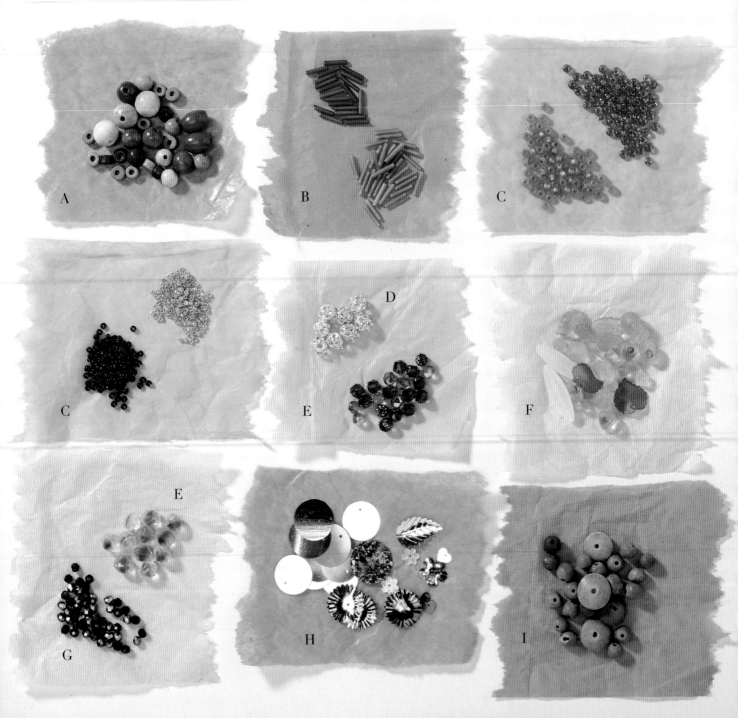

8

Bead types

Anything that can be carved, molded, or drilled can become a bead. Beads come in a wide variety of colors, materials, and shapes, including faceted, round, tube, melon, chips, squares, wafers, and pipes. It would be impossible to define every kind of bead available, but here are a few of the more commonly used ones.

WOODEN (A)
Beads made of wood are lightweight and found in natural and primary colors.

BUGLE (B)
Small tubular glass beads available in a variety of lengths, from small pipes to long straws.

SEED (ROCAILLES) (C)
Tiny, inexpensive glass seed beads in a huge range of colors and finishes. Use a beading needle to thread them.

METAL BEADS (D)
Wirework or metal beads come in many plain or fancy finishes and colors, including ethnic designs.

FACETED BEADS (E)
Faceted glass or plastic beads that reflect the light vary in price; they may be opaque or clear and be of more than one color.

PRESSED GLASS (F)
These beads are stamped into shapes. They are available in many useful shapes, such as hearts, stars, and leaves. They may be clear or opaque.

METALLIC COATED (G)
Coated with metallic paint, these beads can be colored or look like metal.

SEQUINS (H)
Available in many shapes and colors, sequins add glamour and sparkle.

CERAMIC BEADS (I)
Unique, handmade beads that may be plain, painted, or contain colored material.

Technique Tip Beads are available in a range of sizes, 2 mm to 18 mm round being the most common. Small beads increase in size by 1 mm up to 6 mm in diameter and then in 2-mm increments. These sizes are shown in the handy guide below, from left to right.

Collecting and storing

If you keep your eyes open, you will find many sources of cheap or free beads. Unearthing unique and decorative items to turn into beads can become an absorbing hobby in itself.

In addition to buying beads from conventional suppliers (see *Beading Projects*, "Where to buy," page 96), seize any opportunity to find more unusual beads. Secondhand shops, garage sales, antique dealers, and family jewelry castoffs can all harbor interesting and beautiful beads.

All that you need to store beads is a secure receptacle. You can buy specially made compartmentalized boxes, or use old pillboxes or even chocolate boxes. Your box will need a tight lid and several small wells so you can organize your beads by size, color, or type.

Working with color

You may want to store beads according to color, to enable you to create pieces of jewelry or other beadwork within a particular color range.

AVOIDING MONOTONY

To add interest to a single-color piece of work, try to select beads that are very varied in shape or choose a variety of beads in light and dark shades of the same color. You can also use spacers or seed beads in a neutral color to break up solid blocks of a single color.

COMPLEMENTARY COLORS

The traditionally linked complementary colors from opposite sides of the standard color wheel are always a safe bet when coming up with a design. Try conventional pairings such as blue and orange, red and green, yellow and purple, and, for the adventurous,

variations on this theme, such as pink and olive.

SEEING RED

Some cheap beads—particularly those on the red side of the color spectrum—are dyed with a colored varnish that tends to wear off with frequent washing and wear, so buyer beware! If you are designing an item for longevity, choose quality and pay a little more.

The right thread

A variety of threads and wires is available for beadwork—your choice depends on your project. The following can be found in the shops: memory wire, tigertail (nylon-coated wire), nylon thread, leather thong, monofilament, elastic, and cord.

CHOOSING WIRE

Wire (A) for beadwork comes in varying thicknesses and may be colored or plain. Avoid very thin wire, which kinks and breaks easily, and cheap colored wire, as the coating tends to chip and flake off.

Memory wire (B) is sold ready coiled and in different thicknesses. Use for bracelets and necklaces. To use it, you cut off the required length and thread beads onto it.

Tigertail (C) is nylon-coated wire. It has the advantage of being easier to work with than plain wire, but it is difficult to knot, so it requires the use of crimp beads (see page 15).

USING OTHER TYPES OF THREAD

Nylon thread (D) is a good choice when you want a fine, durable thread that is even tougher than natural materials like silk thread. With nylon, you also have a wide choice of color.

Use leather thong (E) for heavier, larger pieces of jewelry. It lends itself well to being knotted and is easy to work with.

Technique Tip Rubbing beeswax (I) along your threads is a good way to prevent them from tangling and becoming frayed. Keep a small block of beeswax, which is available from most craft stores, with the rest of your beading supplies, and apply it to new thread before using it.

If you are looking for an almost invisible thread, monofilament (F) can be a good choice, but bear in mind that it tends to break and stretch, so it is unsuitable for items that are subject to wear and tear.

Elastic (G) is good for children's jewelry, since it's hard-wearing and easily knotted. Cord (H) is another useful thread, available in various widths and finishes.

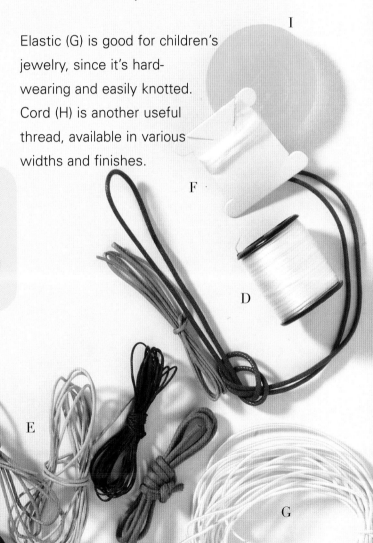

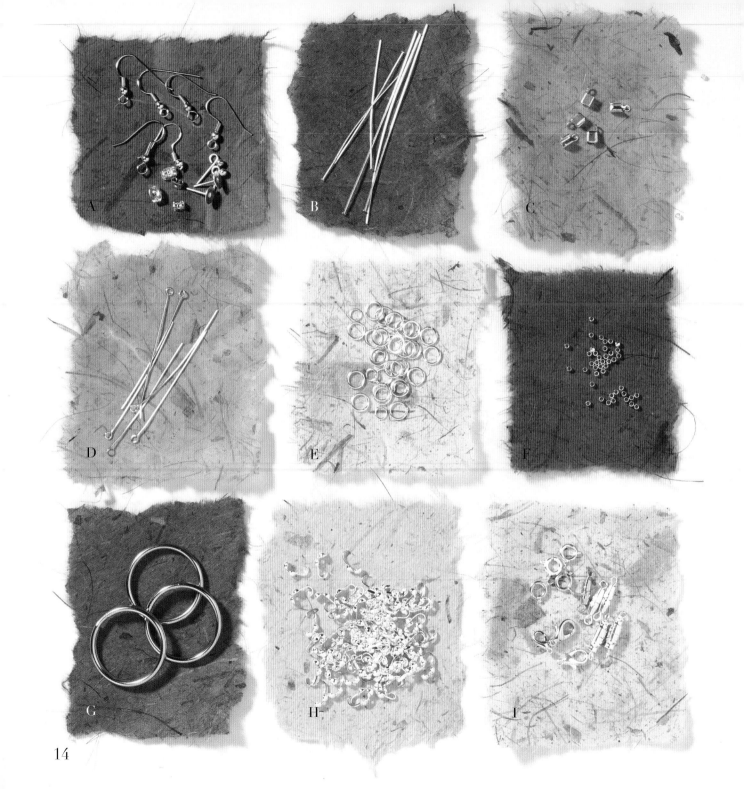

14

Using findings

Findings are the metal mounts, clasps, spacers, and other useful items that are part of the construction of your jewelry. Your choice of findings can alter the whole feel of a piece of beading.

USING CRIMP BEADS

Crimp beads hold things in place on a thread—for example, clasps or other findings. These simple steps (right) show a crimp bead securing a jump ring, but they apply to any project where you want to fix something in place.

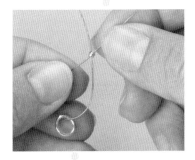

1. Slip a crimp bead and the object to be secured onto the thread; then push the thread back through the crimp bead.

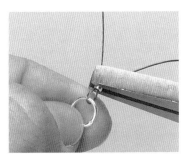

2. Pull the thread tight; then use flat-nose pliers to squash the crimp bead. It now holds the jump ring in place.

ATTACHING LEATHER CRIMPS

Where a crimp is required on a leather thong, you use a leather crimp. This is specially designed to handle the width of the leather. Glue is required to ensure a firm hold.

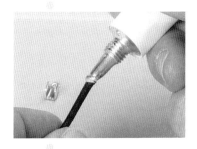

1. Dab a little glue onto the end of a leather thong.

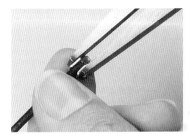

2. Push the leather crimp onto the thong and close it with flat-nose pliers.

FINDINGS: A. Earring hooks, studs, and backs; B. Headpins; C. Leather crimps; D. Eyepins; E. Jump rings; F. Crimp beads; G. Keyring fobs; H. Calottes; I. Clasps.

USING JUMP RINGS

Jump rings are used to join together two different parts of jewelry. They may be open, forming an incomplete circle, or closed, with the ends soldered together.

ATTACHING CALOTTES

Calottes are used to neaten the appearance of your work by hiding unsightly thread ends or crimp beads. They also provide a hook, to which you can fasten a finding.

BENDING HEADPINS

Headpins have a flattened end, like a nail. Eyepins are similar, but have an end loop, to hold more beads. Bending headpins prevents beads from slipping off and gives a neat finish.

To open a jump ring, use round-nose pliers to bend the end of the jump ring toward you, creating a gap in the ring.

1. Add a crimp bead (see page 15). Trim the excess thread; then position the calotte over the bead.

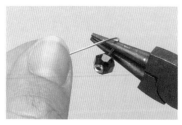

1. Thread your beads onto the headpin. Hold the wire with a pair of flat-nose pliers and bend it over the pliers.

String a closed jump ring onto a thread. Push both ends through a bead and pull tight to hold the ring in place.

2. Make sure the calotte is correctly positioned; then squeeze it with flat-nose pliers to close it.

2. Wrap the wire around itself. To finish, trim the excess wire with wire cutters or scissors.

USING A CALOTTE TO ADD A CLASP

In addition to hiding thread ends or crimp beads, calottes provide a handy hook, to which you can fasten a clasp or any other findings.

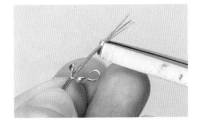

1. Add a calotte and a crimp bead to a number of threads and close the calotte (see "Attaching calottes," page 16).

2. Trim the excess and then hook a fastening onto the calotte. With flat-nose pliers, close the hook of the calotte.

USING A CRIMP BEAD TO ADD A FASTENING

For a different look to your jewelry, you can omit the calotte (above) and simply finish off the piece with a crimp bead.

1. Add a crimp bead and a fastening to the thread and pull the thread back through the crimp bead.

2. Pull the crimp bead down tight into position and close it with pliers (see page 15). Trim the excess thread.

OTHER FINDINGS

Some findings not used in this book are illustrated at left. They include rings, ring and bar fastenings, bead cups, chains, leather crimps, spiral cages, and brooch backs.

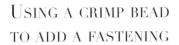

Choosing your tools

One of the nice things about beading is that you don't need a lot of specialized equipment—a square of felt or chamois leather and a pair of pliers may be all that is required.

Bead board
Although you can make do with a simple square of material on which to lay out your beads, you can go one better and buy a bead board. These are specially made and often have storage compartments to hold your beads while you work. Their grooves are designed to allow you to try combining different colors and shapes before stringing them onto a piece of jewelry.

Whether you choose a piece of cloth, a bead board, or a simple tray, make sure your solution prevents your beads from getting lost and allows you some degree of mobility.

Beading needles
If you are using many small beads—for example, seed (rocaille) beads—a beading needle can make your task easier. Beading needles are long and fine, enabling you to pick up and thread small beads easily.

Pliers

Two types of pliers are often used in beading. Flat-nose pliers are used to crush crimp beads onto thread or to squeeze the ends of wire together. Round-nose pliers are useful when you don't want to squash the item you are manipulating—for example, when shaping wire spirals and loops in pins.

Glue

Sometimes, a dab of glue can be just what is needed to secure a jewelry component—for an example, see "Attaching leather crimps," on page 15.

Hardware

A bead reemer is extremely useful for unblocking or enlarging holes in beads. Scissors will give the ends of your thread a clean finish, while a small hammer, masking tape, and a ruler will also come in handy for general work.

Tweezers and magnifying glass

If you are working with small beads and findings, a good pair of tweezers and a magnifying glass may help. For detailed work, tweezers must be fine enough to allow you to pick up small beads easily. A magnifying glass can be useful for detailed work, but the best purchase is one on a stand, which leaves both hands free to work.

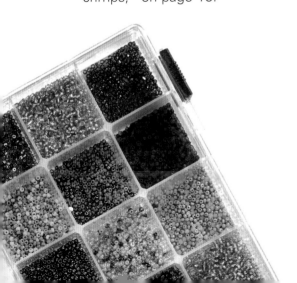

Designing with beads

When starting out, try to keep things simple. Use a bead board (see page 18) to experiment with different patterns and colors before you start stringing your beads. Tape thread ends to a work surface or use a slip knot (see page 24) to prevent the beads from escaping.

SYMMETRICAL PATTERNS

A symmetrical design can be useful for formal, structured pieces. When arranging a symmetrical pattern, start with the central bead or combination of beads, and work outward toward the ends. Remember to leave enough room on the thread for a clasp or fastening.

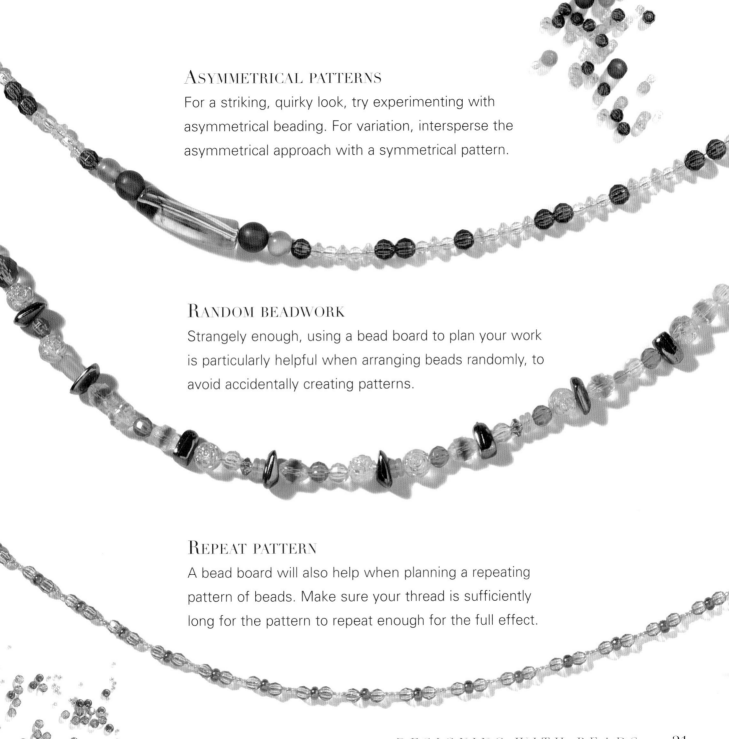

ASYMMETRICAL PATTERNS

For a striking, quirky look, try experimenting with asymmetrical beading. For variation, intersperse the asymmetrical approach with a symmetrical pattern.

RANDOM BEADWORK

Strangely enough, using a bead board to plan your work is particularly helpful when arranging beads randomly, to avoid accidentally creating patterns.

REPEAT PATTERN

A bead board will also help when planning a repeating pattern of beads. Make sure your thread is sufficiently long for the pattern to repeat enough for the full effect.

Simple weaving

Although weaving with beads is slightly more complex than stringing them, you need to learn only the simple techniques described here to be able to make many eye-catching objects.

FRINGING

A useful and decorative way of finishing off many items, fringing is a simple technique. For variety, try adding more beads on the end of each strand or missing a bead at the beginning of each one, to give a wider-spaced fringe.

BRICK STITCH

Brick stitch (commanche weave) looks like peyote stitch (see opposite). Because the thread is looped back through each bead, it takes time to complete but is very stable. Repeat until you achieve the desired size.

1. Thread the sequence of beads that will form a single strand of the fringe and loop back through the final bead.

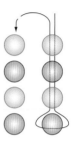

2. Thread back through the sequence. Go through the next bead (not shown); then start the next strand of fringe.

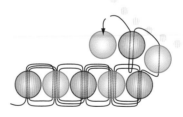

1. Start a ladder row by looping two beads together twice. Add the next bead, also with a double loop. Continue to the row end. Add a bead and take the thread through the first loop of the ladder.

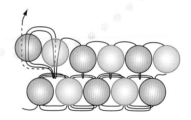

2. Repeat down the row. Loop through the last bead twice; then add one bead and pass the thread through the first loop of the last row.

Peyote

A popular and flexible technique, peyote stitch is easiest with uniform-sized and -shaped beads. These steps (at right) are for a rectangle with an odd number of beads per row, but peyote can be adapted to fit any shape.

Burying ends

For a neat finish to your work, it is important to learn how to bury the ends of the thread securely. You can either do this as you go or leave it until you've finished.

Technique Tip To make weaving easier and to avoid kinks and knots in your thread, apply beeswax before you start your work.

1. Tie a knot in the end of the thread, add one bead, and loop back through it to act as a stopper. String five beads onto the thread.

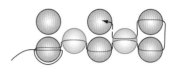

2. Add a bead to begin the next row; then take the thread back through the last blue bead in the previous row. Repeat down the row.

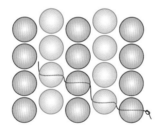

1. Tie an overhand knot (see page 24) around the existing thread and pass the thread back through four beads.

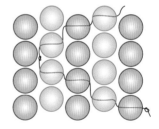

2. Repeat, passing the thread through more beads. For a secure finish, seal the knots with a dab of glue.

Know your knots

You need to learn only a few simple knots to ensure that your beading projects are finished off securely. Choosing the right knot comes with practice, but here are a few guidelines.

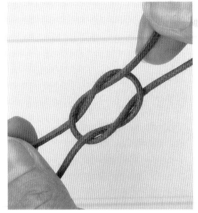

SLIP KNOT

Use a slip knot for temporary tying—for example, to secure the ends of the thread while stringing beads. You then have the option of changing your mind or permanently fixing the end.

SQUARE KNOT

To tie two threads together, a square knot is a good choice. To tie this knot, take one end under the other and pull until the knot is in the right place. Repeat and pull on the ends to tighten and secure the knot.

OVERHAND KNOT

You can use simple overhand knots as a less conspicuous alternative to crimp beads to hold beads in place on a thread. Make a loop, take one end of the thread through the loop, and pull it tight.

OVERHAND KNOT WITH LOOP

A type of the overhand knot can form a loop to make part of a simple fastening. Instead of taking one end of the thread through the loop, pass a second loop through the first and pull it tight.

WEAVER'S KNOT

If you need to join threads during woven beadwork, a weaver's knot can be the answer. If you choose the right thread, it forms a neat-enough knot to hide easily inside a bead and will hold your work together securely.

LARK'S HEAD KNOT

The knot commonly used to secure a chunky bead or amulet on a thong is the lark's head knot. It has many other uses in jewelry beadwork and is tied by passing both ends of a thread through a loop.

Working with wire

Learning basic wirework techniques is an important part of making bead jewelry. Once you have mastered a few simple procedures, you will be able to produce beautiful and original bracelets, necklaces, and earrings.

MAKING A LOOP

Wire loops are used extensively in beaded jewelry. They can hold dangly beads or other striking pieces of jewelry.

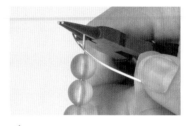

1. With a bead threaded, grasp the wire with round-nose pliers and bend it over.

2. Use either fingers or pliers to bend the wire around itself. Trim the excess wire.

MAKING A SPIRAL

You can make a neat and attractive end to your jewelry once you have learned how to make a spiral. Your first attempt will probably not be perfect, but your technique will improve with practice.

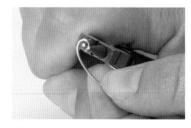

1. Bend the wire over the top of a pair of round-nose pliers. Keep your grip on the wire with the pliers.

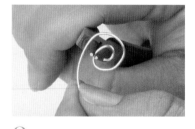

2. Bend the wire around the pliers to form a spiral. You may need to modify your grip to achieve the perfect spiral.

TWISTING

To hold beads neatly and decoratively in place, learn the simple technique of twisting wire.

1. Thread a bead on a wire and bend the ends of the wire toward each other.

2. Use either your fingers or round-nose pliers to twist one end around the other.

MEMORY WIRE

Many types of jewelry can be easily produced from memory wire. It is sold ready coiled—all you need to do is add beads and secure the ends.

1. Secure one end by bending it, taping it, or using a crimp bead. Thread beads.

2. Trim any excess wire and bend over the end with round-nose pliers to finish.

HAMMERING

You can produce attractive and interesting effects by flattening wire. Hammering can also hold beads in place without using crimps or knots.

1. Thread your beads onto the wire, and on a flat metal surface or anvil, hammer the part of the wire to be flattened.

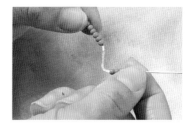

2. Add more beads. The flattened area holds the beads in place without the need for crimp beads or knots.

Wire jewelry ideas

The first wire beading project tackled by many novice beaders is simple wire earrings, but with a little practice, you will be able to make many other exciting pieces.

EARRINGS

For really simple earrings, you can thread beads onto a headpin or eyepin, bend the end with round-nose pliers, and attach appropriate findings.

Attractive earrings can also be made from ready-made hoops, spirals, chains, large single crystal drops, or drilled coins.

For making earrings, be sure you have a selection of specialized findings, including kidney wire or ear posts or studs, and ear clips or screws for nonpierced ears.

NECKLACES

Beaded eyepins can also be strung together end to end, to make a necklace. Other types of necklace could include memory wire, chains, beads knotted on a thread, pendants, chokers, and crystal drops.

Try experimenting with new types of beads and fastenings—attractive necklaces have come from materials as diverse and unusual as balloons and pasta!

BRACELETS

Most bracelets are constructed in a similar way to necklaces and are often part of a matching set. However, wire bangles and charm bracelets tend to be one-of-a-kind pieces.

For both necklaces and bracelets, unless you are going to content yourself with simple wire loops to finish off your jewelry, be sure you have a good selection of appropriate findings, such as bolt rings, hooks, and barrel clasps.

RINGS

Simple rings can be made from beaded spirals or single loops of appropriately sized wire. You can even buy ring bases with loops, ready for you to attach your own selection of decorative beads. Smaller beads are usually suitable for rings, although you may be able to create a striking piece by combining a single dramatic large bead with a few complementary smaller ones.

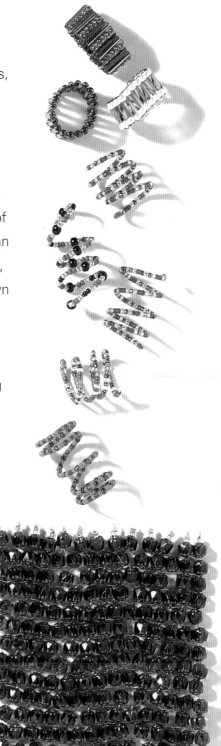

Embroidering with beads

An ordinary-looking piece of fabric can be given a beautifully jeweled, exotic, or luxurious air with the addition of a few well-chosen beads or sequins. Knowing how is the key.

EMBROIDERY EQUIPMENT

To begin with, you probably won't need any equipment in addition to that which you already have around the house. A good pair of scissors, a few needles chosen to reflect the weight of the thread and the size of the holes of the beads you have chosen, thread, fabric, and perhaps an embroidery hoop will suffice. If you progress to working with smaller beads, you will need a long, fine beading needle, available from a general needlecrafts store.

Stitching techniques

Traditional embroidery stitches can be embellished with seed, bugle, or larger beads to create densely textured and brightly colored patterns to decorate soft furnishings or fashion accessories.

LAZY DAISY STITCH

This pretty stitch is made up of eight detached chain stitches, worked in a circle to create a simple flower shape. It can be embellished with a small bead at the tip of each petal or a larger bead or sequin in the center. Work it in rows, singly as a feature stitch, or embroider several "daisies" in a cluster to make an entire posy. You may want to draw a circle with a fabric marker before starting work, to be sure that the petals are evenly spaced.

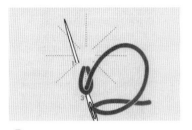

1. Bring the needle out at 1. Loop the thread to the right; then insert the needle at 1. Bring the point out directly below, at 2.

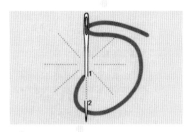

2. Pull the needle through to form an oval loop. Make a short stitch at 3 to hold the loop. Start the next petal at 4 and repeat the process.

3. Make six more stitches to complete the flower.

FLY STITCH

A versatile stitch, resembling the letter Y, fly stitch can be worked in vertical or horizontal rows to create geometric patterns, or at random, as a background or filling.

Seed beads, sewn at the tips or the point, will add highlights of color and bugle beads can be sewn into a zigzag line to echo the shape of the stitches.

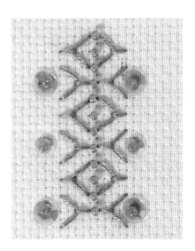

1. Bring the needle up at 1; then take it across to the right, at 2. Bring the point out at 3, centrally below the first two points. Pull the needle through gently, over the looped thread.

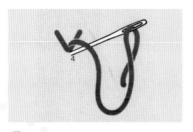

2. Complete the Y by taking the needle back down at 4 to make a short, straight, tying stitch.

3. For a textured background or filling, work more stitches at closely spaced but random intervals.

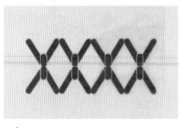

4. Fly stitch can be arranged to form geometric patterns.

1. Bring the needle up at 1. Insert it at 2, to the right, and bring the needle through over the looped thread at 3.

2. Insert the needle at 4. Bring the point out down to the right at 5 and pull the needle through over the loop.

3. Make the second stitch from 6 to 7 (directly below 4) and pull the needle through.

4. Insert the needle at 8, below 3, and across from 7. Pass it over the thread, at 9.

5. The final stitch is worked directly below the first stitch.

6. Repeat as required, from 1 to 9. Finish with a short stitch over the final loop.

DOUBLE FEATHER STITCH

This pretty looped border stitch forms a wide, flexible line, which is useful for depicting leafy foliage. It is traditionally used to decorate the silk and satin patches of elaborate crazy patchwork and also on children's garments.

Seed beads can be added to the branches for a really elaborate finish.

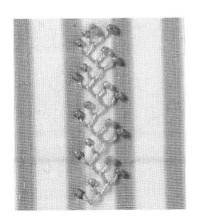

Attaching beads

Beads, small or large, are useful as highlights with embroidered designs or for picking out details on a patterned background fabric. They can be used singly or sewn down in short rows (bead satin stitch) to imitate weaving.

ROUND BEADS

To sew down a single bead, bring up the needle, thread on the bead, then take the needle back down, exactly the bead's width from the start point. For a secure finish, work another stitch through the hole.

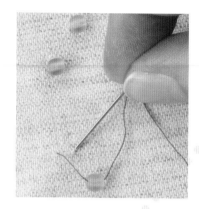

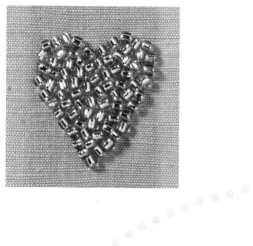

For bead satin stitch, bring up the needle at the top-left corner and thread on up to five small beads. Lay them downward across the fabric and take the needle down at the end of the row, making sure that the strand is taut. Work the following rows a single bead's width apart.

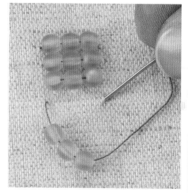

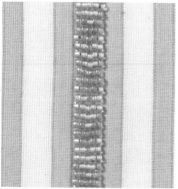

COUCHING

This stitch is used to create flowing lines made up from strands of seed beads, such as monograms and curved outlines. Draw the required line onto the fabric with a marker pen. Thread a needle with a double length of thread and bring it up at the start of the line. Add enough small beads to cover its length.

Bring a second thread up on the line, just below the first bead, and make a small stitch to anchor down the double thread. Repeat this couching stitch to the end of the line, ensuring that the beads lie exactly over it.

BUGLE BEADS

To sew a single bead, bring up the needle, thread on a single bead, then take it down close to the end of the bead. Form a solid line by stitching the beads side by side or at alternate angles for a zigzag. To attach a whole row of bugles, thread them on and take the needle through to the back. Come up between the first and second beads and make a tiny stitch to hold the thread in place. Repeat as necessary.

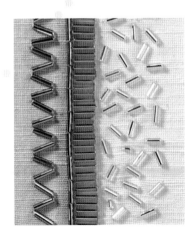

SINGLE SEQUIN

Sequins are available in many interesting cut-out shapes as well as the usual flat and cupped circles. Smaller sequins usually have a center hole: Sew them down with a single stitch from the center outward. Larger ones have several smaller holes around the edge. Make a small stitch in each hole, using a matching sewing thread.

SEQUIN STAR

To make the stitches into a feature, use a contrasting thread and work five straight stitches from the center outward, spacing them evenly and extending them just beyond the edge of the sequin.

OVERLAPPING SEQUINS

Flat round sequins can be sewn down in overlapping rows, like fish scales, concealing the thread. Sew the first sequin down with a short stitch from the center outward, worked in the direction of the line. Come up again a sequin's width from the start. Add a second sequin; then take the needle down at the edge of the first. Continue making back stitches in this way to the end of the line.

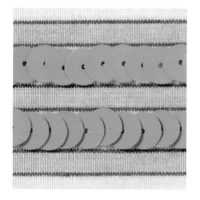

SEQUINS AND BEADS

The prettiest way to attach a sequin is to hold it down with a seed bead. This works best with cup- or flower-shaped sequins. Bring up the needle, thread on the sequin followed by a small bead, then take it back down through the sequin hole. As ever, a second stitch will make it more secure.

DROP BEADS

Pear- or teardrop-shaped beads, with a hole through the tip, work well in bead embroidery. They cannot be stitched directly to the fabric because of their rounded shape, but they are usually attached with a loop of small beads. Bring up the needle, thread on five seed beads followed by the main bead and three more seed beads. Take the needle back through the first two beads and back through the starting point.

JEWELRY STONES OR DIAMANTÉS

These faceted glass jewels are always used to add glitz and glitter. Small clips attach them to a flat metal backing, which is crossed by two grooves. Sew them down by making two stitches through each of the grooves, starting and ending each stitch as close as possible to the metal to conceal the thread.

Beads to make or find

In addition to buying beads from the huge variety available from craft stores and beading suppliers, you may want to consider making your own, to create that really special, one-of-a-kind design. As you can turn almost anything into a bead, the choice is limited only by your imagination.

POLYMER CLAY

Inexpensive and versatile, polymer clay comes in a range of colors and can be shaped as you please. It can be fired in the oven, usually in under half an hour.

CLAY AND CERAMIC

Similar to polymer clay, but not quite as convenient and easy to use, these also lend themselves well to beads.

FELTED BEADS

Make your own felted beads by rolling small balls of unspun wool (known as wool roving) in soap flakes, first in hot, then cold water, until felting occurs.

PAPER BEADS

Beads made from rolled paper or papier-mâché can be as sophisticated or simple as you want. A popular technique is to roll strips of colored paper around a small cylinder such as a toothpick.

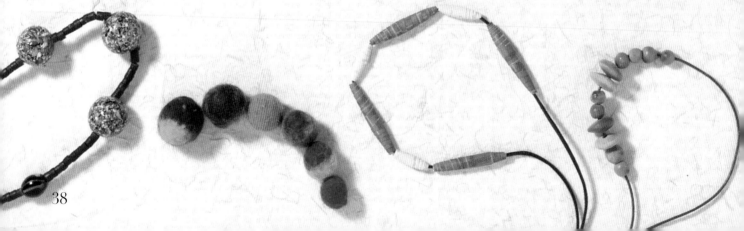

Wood and bone

Beautiful beads can be fashioned from raw or polished wood. Even lengths of bamboo or untreated pine can be made into beautiful, striking pieces. And if ivory is hard to find or out of your price range, you can use other types of bone for a similar effect, such as animal teeth or larger fish bones.

Other found objects

Many other ordinary objects can be adapted to make attractive beads. Food items, such as pasta shapes, colorful sweets, and nuts all have their place, particularly in bright necklaces for children. Other household items to try include corks, buttons, rolled strips of cloth, colored paper clips, and old keys.

Shells

Light, easily cleaned and drilled, shells are ideal homemade beads. Try to collect shells of similar size, species, or color to give uniformity to your design.

Forming holes

You can make a hole in many found objects or homemade beads with an ordinary darning needle. If your found object is too hard for this, try drilling it with a small electric or hand drill, using a very fine bit.

Index